Olga and the Stork

Written by Joe Hackett
Illustrated by Natalie Hinrichsen

WAYLAND

Bump, bump, bump, rattled the bus as it went over the stony road.

Olga sighed. She hated leaving the city to visit her nana in the village. Everything was just too... old!

At last the bus rolled into the village square. Olga said goodbye to mum, got her bag and climbed off the bus, feeling tired, hot and a little bit cross!

Her nana was waiting for her in the same spot as always.

"Olga, my dear, I've got a present for you!" Nana cried, giving Olga a hug and a rather sloppy kiss.

Olga hated being kissed by Nana, who had whiskers on her chin, but the idea of a present cheered her up.

"What is it?" Olga asked, holding out her hand.

"It's a special bracelet," said Nana, as she tied a small red and white woollen bracelet onto Olga's wrist.

"Thanks," whispered Olga, trying not to look disappointed. "Why is it so special, Nana?"

"It's a custom. All girls in the village wear a bracelet until the stork arrives. It always comes, every year, on 21st March," said Nana.

"I have to wear the bracelet for three weeks!" cried Olga.

"Yes, and then, when you see the stork, you cut off the bracelet and tie it to a fruit tree to make the fruit grow well," Nana explained.

"Oh, I see," said Olga, looking at the bracelet, but she didn't really see why it was so important. The woollen bracelet seemed like another one of Nana's silly old customs.

Nana and Olga walked home. The winter snow had melted at last and the sun was shining. A donkey, goats, chickens and dogs roamed free in the fields.

Olga didn't notice any of the animals.
She dragged her bag along the ground
and wished she was back at home in the
city, playing on her computer.

"Olga, please don't be miserable. You should be proud of our village and its Bulgarian customs," Nana insisted.

"I am, Nana," Olga mourned, "but sometimes I wish there was more to do here."

The next day, all Olga wanted to do was play with her games console.

"Why don't you feed the chickens?" asked Nana. "Enjoy the fresh air!"

18

"Oh, no," explained Olga. "This is much more fun. Look! You can make the little men fight."

"Ach! I have no time for that modern nonsense. I have too much work to do," complained Nana.

So Olga took the game round to Mitra's house next door. Mitra had never seen such a thing!

"Can I have a go?" Mitra asked.

"All right, but be careful. It's expensive," said Olga.

As Mitra reached to take the games console, Olga saw Mitra's bracelet.

"We have matching bracelets!" Olga cried.

"White is for a long life and red is for good health," Mitra explained, proudly showing off her bracelet.

"Where does the stork come from?"
asked Olga, the games console
suddenly forgotten.

"From far away. Each spring it returns
to its nest on the telephone pole near
the river," said Mitra. "Come on, I'll
show you!"

Mitra and Olga ran to the telephone pole. There at the very top was a big straggly, empty nest.

"Nana says the stork always returns on the same day," Olga said. "How can it always be exactly the same day, every year?"

"I don't know," said Mitra,
"but it always is."

As the days got warmer, Olga and Mitra went out to the telephone pole to wait for the stork, just in case it came early!

"I thought you didn't like our Bulgarian customs," said Nana, as Olga ran out of the front door straight after breakfast. "What about your game?"

"But it's 21st March today. The stork will be here! Come on, Nana! I don't have time to play my games console," cried Olga.

So Olga and Nana set off to meet the stork. Sure enough, they soon saw a huge bird with black and white wings flying down the valley towards them.

The stork landed on the empty nest
and gave a loud, "Awk".

"It's here! It's here," shouted Olga,
jumping up and down. "You were
right, Nana."

"I always know best!" laughed Nana.
"Come on, let's go and find a fruit tree..."

START READING is a series of highly enjoyable books for beginner readers. **The books have been carefully graded to match the Book Bands widely used in schools.** This enables readers to be sure they choose books that match their own reading ability.

**Look out for the Band colour on the book
in our Start Reading logo.**

The Bands are:

| Pink Band 1A & 1B |
| Red Band 2 |
| Yellow Band 3 |
| Blue Band 4 |
| Green Band 5 |
| Orange Band 6 |
| Turquoise Band 7 |
| Purple Band 8 |
| Gold Band 9 |

START READING books can be read independently or shared with an adult. They promote the enjoyment of reading through satisfying stories, plays and non-fiction narratives, which are supported by fun illustrations and photographs.

Joe Hackett often visits a village in Bulgaria — one of his favourite countries —because the people are friendly and there's a lot of wildlife to see. He hasn't yet spotted a wolf but he knows they are up there in the forests and mountains somewhere!

Natalie Hinrichsen works in her loft studio in a suburb of Cape Town, South Africa. She has been illustrating children's books since 1996 and in 2005 she won the Vivian Wilkes award for illustration.